DRAGON MASTERS

EYE OF THE EARTHQUAKE DRAGON

BY

TRACEY WEST

SCHOLASTIC INC.

DRAGON MASTERS

Read All the Adventures

TABLE OF CONTENTS

THIS BOOK GOES OUT TO MY BROTHER,
Michael, because as Zelda knows, things are better when you have one. — TW

Library of Congress Cataloging-in-Publication Data
Names: West, Tracey, 1965- author. Griffo, Daniel, illustrator. West, Tracey, 1965- Dragon Masters ; 13.
Title: Eye of the Earthquake Dragon / by Tracey West ; illustrated by Daniel Griffo.
Description: First edition. New York, NY : Branches/Scholastic Inc., 2019. Series: Dragon masters ; 13
Summary: The evil wizard Maldred has stolen the gold and silver keys which will allow him to release the Naga, the powerful Earthquake Dragon at the center of the earth--so Drake and several of the other Dragon Masters travel to the Naga's Temple in the Dragon Islands, to try and stop Maldred, and prevent him and the Earthquake Dragon from destroying the kingdom.
Identifiers: LCCN 2018017047 ISBN 9781338263718 (pbk : alk. paper)
ISBN 9781338263725 (hardcover : alk. paper)
Subjects: LCSH: Dragons—Juvenile fiction. Magic—Juvenile fiction. Wizards—Juvenile fiction. Locks and keys—Juvenile fiction. Adventure stories. CYAC: Dragons—Fiction. Magic—Fiction. Wizards—Fiction. Locks and keys—Fiction. Adventure and adventurers—Fiction. LCGFT: Action and adventure fiction.
Classification: LCC PZ7.W51937 Ew 2019 DDC 813.54 [Fic] —dc23 LC record available at https://lccn.loc.gov/2018017047

10 9 8 7 6 5 4 3 2 1 19 20 21 22 23

Printed in China 62
First edition, May 2019
Illustrated by Daniel Griffo
Edited by Katie Carella
Book design by Sarah Dvojack

MALDRED HAS THE KEYS!

Flash! A bright green light shimmered in the underground training room in King Roland's castle.

Four Dragon Masters and their dragons appeared out of thin air. Drake and his Earth Dragon, Worm. Rori and her Fire Dragon, Vulcan. Jean and her Silver Dragon, Argent. And Darma and his Gold Dragon, Hema.

Drake blinked as the green light faded. The light came from his dragon. Worm had strong mind powers that transported them from one place to another.

"Thank you, Worm," Drake said as the green Dragon Stone he wore around his neck glowed.

All Dragon Masters wore one. It allowed them to communicate with their dragons.

Drake heard Worm's reply inside his mind: *You are welcome.*

"Please bring the other dragons to the Dragon Caves to get some food and water," Drake told Worm. "We will stay here and report to Griffith."

Worm nodded. Then Vulcan, Argent, and Hema followed him out of the Training Room.

Drake looked around. Wizards filled the room! He spotted Griffith, King Roland's wizard, who taught him and some of the other Dragon Masters.

"Griffith!" Drake called out.

A tall wizard with a long white beard walked up to him.

"Hello, Drake and Rori," Griffith said. "Can you introduce me to the new Dragon Masters?"

"This is Jean, the protector of the Silver Key," Drake said. "And Darma, the protector of the Gold Key."

Drake had met Jean and Darma on a mission to stop Maldred, a dark wizard. Maldred was plotting to steal two keys that would give him control of a huge dragon with the power to destroy the world: the Naga.

When the Naga hatched a long time ago, he didn't understand his own powers. He created powerful earthquakes. So wizards made a Silver Key and a Gold Key to lock the Naga away. The keys had been guarded safely for years . . . until now.

"Griffith, we have a big problem!" Rori blurted out. "Maldred has stolen both keys!"

"We've got to stop him before he unlocks the power of the Naga!" Jean cried.

"Maldred may have the keys, but he has not reached the Naga yet," Griffith explained calmly. "These wizards have cast a spell on Maldred."

Drake looked around the room. The wizards were standing in a circle now.

Drake recognized one of them — Hulda, a wizard from the Far North. She and the other wizards were pointing at a glass globe floating in the middle of the circle. Magic flowed from their fingertips.

Inside the globe, Drake saw an image of Maldred. He was standing still, like a statue.

"Right now, the wizards have trapped Maldred in a magical dimension," Griffith said. "While he's there, he is unable to move or use his powers."

Darma spoke for the first time, smiling. "That is good," he said.

"But the wizards cannot keep Maldred frozen for long," Griffith warned.

"We need to act fast!" Rori cried. "Before Maldred breaks out and goes after the Naga!"

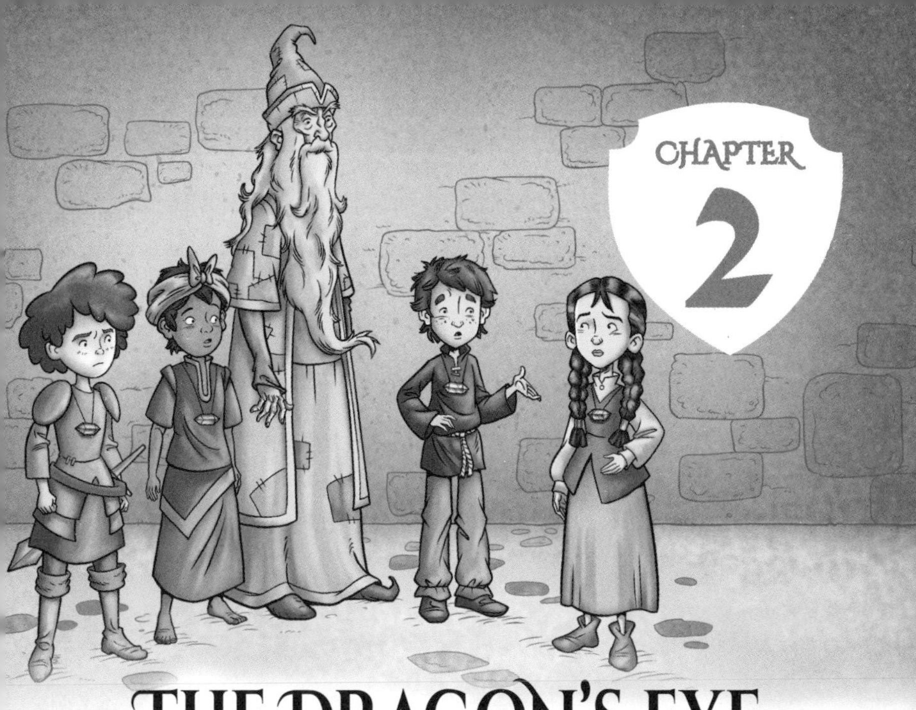

THE DRAGON'S EYE

"How much time do we have?" Jean asked Griffith.

"Not much. We expect that Maldred will break out of our spell soon," Griffith replied. "But the wizards and I are crafting a new spell that will stop him for good. The other Dragon Masters are helping us prepare it."

Drake looked around. "Are they here?"

Griffith shook his head. "Bo and Ana are gathering important items for our spell," he explained. "And Petra is searching her family's library for a special book."

"Are you sure the new spell will work?" Rori asked. "Maldred already broke out of Wizard's Council Prison once."

"This spell is much more powerful than wizard's prison," Griffith promised.

Darma spoke up. "While you are busy crafting the spell, perhaps some of us could try to find the Naga," he said. He held out a piece of paper with a map stamped on it in ink.

Griffith's eyes widened. "Is that a map?"

"Yes," Drake answered. "Maldred might have got the keys, but Darma got this from him."

"Maldred figured out that the raised markings on the keys created this map," Darma said. "He said these shapes are islands."

"Indeed they are," the wizard said. "This is a map of the Dragon Islands!"

"Maldred said this map showed him where to find the Naga," Jean said.

"But I don't understand. How do we know exactly where the Naga is?" Rori asked.

"Follow me to the classroom," Griffith said.

The four Dragon Masters walked past the circle of wizards into the classroom. Griffith picked up a book.

"I have been searching for clues about where the Naga might live," he said. "I found this rhyme." He began to read out loud.

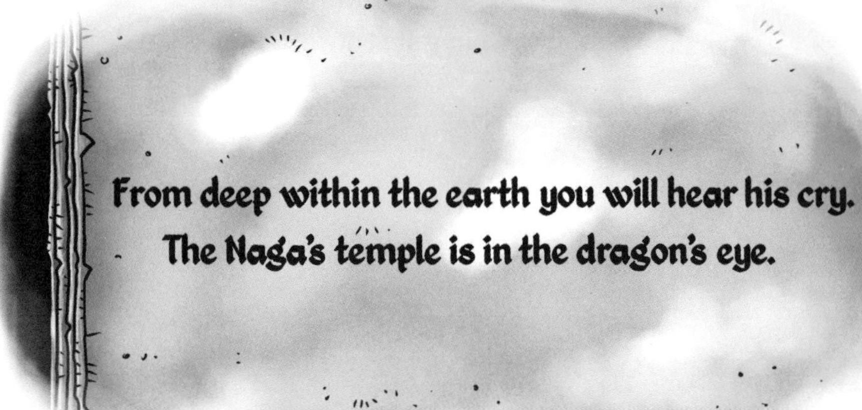

From deep within the earth you will hear his cry.
The Naga's temple is in the dragon's eye.

"The dragon's eye?" Rori repeated.

Darma laid the map on the table. Drake could see now that the islands made the shape of a dragon. The dragon had a head, a body, a tail, and legs.

Jean pointed to a dot on the map. “Look! That dot is where a dragon’s eye would be.”

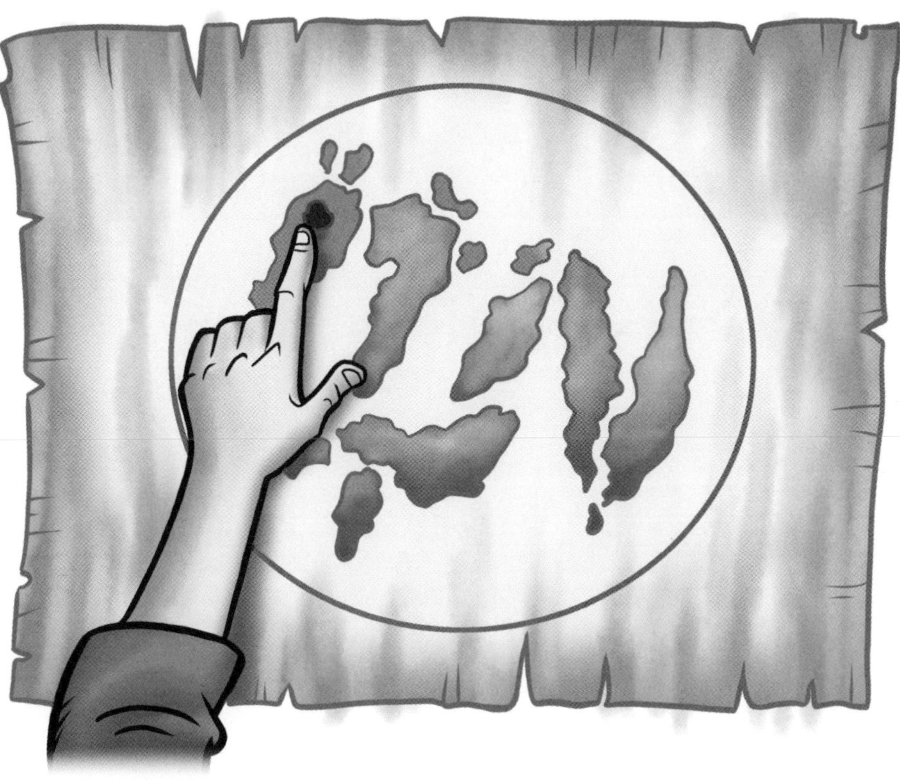

Griffith took a closer look. “You are right!” he said. He turned to Drake. “You must travel to the eye of the Dragon Islands. Find the temple of the Naga before Maldred does!”

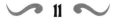

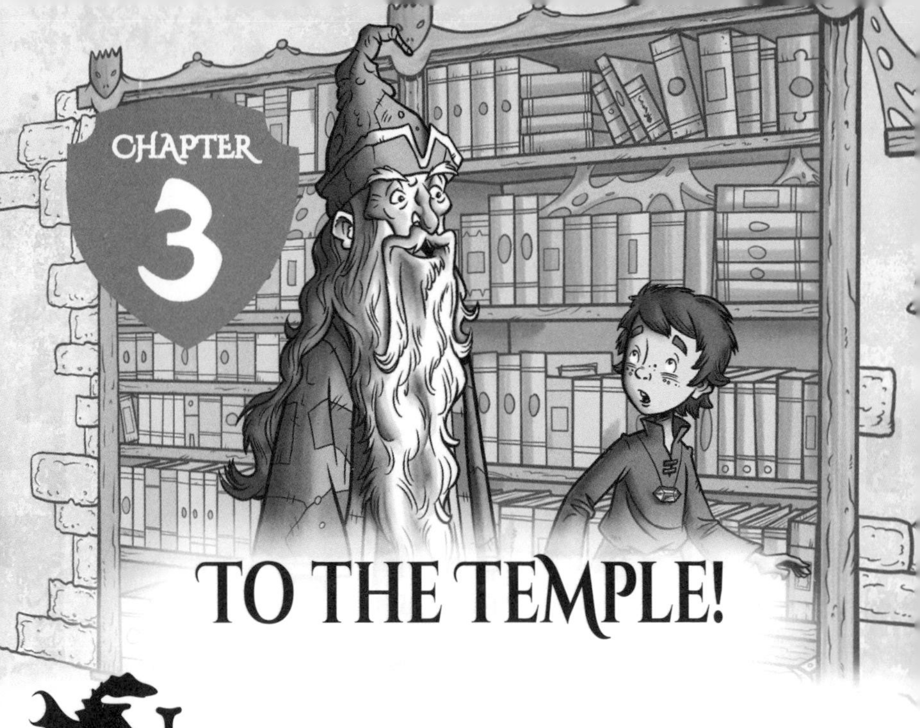

TO THE TEMPLE!

"Now that we know where the Dragon Islands are, Worm can take us there in a flash," Drake said. "But what should we do when we get there?"

"You must warn the Naga's Dragon Master that Maldred is on his way," Griffith replied.

"Wait," Jean said. "The Naga has a Dragon Master?"

"Yes. But the legend of the Naga does not tell any more about his master," Griffith said.

"Did you ask the Dragon Stone?" Drake asked.

Griffith had a large green chunk of the Dragon Stone in his workshop. The Dragon Stone chose a Dragon Master for each dragon.

"I did," Griffith replied. "But the picture it showed me was cloudy. There is very strong magic surrounding the Naga."

Drake tried to imagine what the Naga's Dragon Master might look like. *You'd have to be big and strong to control such a powerful dragon,* he guessed. *I bet the Naga's Dragon Master is a grown-up, not eight years old, like me and my friends.*

"We'll warn the Naga's Dragon Master about Maldred," Rori said. Then she made a fist. "And if that evil wizard shows up, we'll make sure that he doesn't get control of the Naga!"

Griffith shook his head. "Rori, I need you to stay here," he said. "Every important wizard in the world is in this castle. If Maldred gets free and decides to attack, we will need all the help we can get."

Rori nodded. "That is true," she said. "Vulcan and I will guard the castle."

"Thank you, Rori," Griffith said. He turned to Darma and Jean. "You two will go with Drake."

I'm glad my new friends are going with me, Drake thought. *I know I can learn a lot from them.*

"We will do our best to protect the world from the Naga," Darma promised.

"I know you will!" Griffith said. Then he walked to a shelf and picked up two small, round mirrors. He gave one to Drake.

"Take this magic mirror with you," Griffith said. "You can use it to contact me. And I can contact you with mine."

"Thanks," Drake said, slipping it into his belt next to his silver sword. Jean had given him the sword in the lair of the Silver Dragon.

"We had better go now," Jean said.

Drake, Jean, and Darma said good-bye to Griffith and Rori. Then they rushed to the Dragon Caves.

Drake showed Worm the map and pointed to the eye of the Dragon Islands. "Can you get us to the Naga's temple?"

The green Dragon Stone around Drake's neck began to glow. Drake heard Worm's voice in his head: *Yes.*

Drake touched Worm's neck. Jean and Darma each put one hand on Worm, and one hand on their dragons.

"To the temple!" Drake cried.

UNDERGROUND

Drake's stomach flip-flopped as Worm transported them to the island. When the dragon's green glow faded, Drake blinked.

At first, he couldn't see anything except darkness.

"Hema, please shine for us," Darma told the Gold Dragon.

"Argent, you, too," Jean told the Silver Dragon.

The two dragons began to shine with silver and gold light.

Drake gasped as the metallic lights swirled together, sparkling in the darkness. *That's beautiful!* he thought.

"We're underground," Darma said.

"Is this the temple?" Drake asked.

"It doesn't look like the inside of a temple," Jean said. She pointed to a tunnel in front of them. "Maybe the temple's down there."

Hema and Argent lit the way as they walked through the tunnel.

Drake looked at Darma and Jean. "I'm glad you two are with me," he confessed.

"I must be here because it is my sworn duty to protect the Silver Key," Jean said. "But I'm glad that you are here with us, Drake."

"As am I," Darma added. "There is a reason that fate brought the three of us together. I believe we will not fail."

"I hope you're right," Drake said.

Soon the tunnel opened up into an enormous space.

Drake gazed around in wonder. The floor was made of smooth, dark stone. A very, very long dragon was painted across each wall. At the far end of the space, Drake could see a large ball of glowing yellow energy.

Slowly, the three Dragon Masters and their dragons moved closer to the ball of light.

Two figures were floating inside the bright ball. One was a boy with pure white hair, dressed all in white. The other was a girl with dark black hair, dressed all in black. Each of them was wearing a Dragon Stone.

"Those are Dragon Masters!" Drake cried.

CHAPTER 5

TWO DRAGON MASTERS?

"Why are Dragon Masters floating in a ball of yellow light?" Jean wondered aloud.

"Maybe they need our help," Drake guessed.

"I do not think these Dragon Masters need saving," Darma said.

As Darma spoke, the yellow light began to fade. The two Dragon Masters gently floated to the ground. Their eyes narrowed as they stared at Drake, Darma, and Jean.

"Who dares to enter the Temple of the Naga?" they asked, talking at the same time.

"I am Drake, and this is Darma and Jean," Drake said. "We're Dragon Masters, too." He pulled out his Dragon Stone necklace and showed it to them.

"I didn't know a dragon could have two masters," Jean added. "Are you *both* Dragon Masters of the Naga?"

The boy and girl didn't answer Jean's question.

"Intruders are not allowed in the temple," they said.

They held out their arms. Streams of yellow light snaked from their fingertips. The yellow light sped toward Drake and the others.

"Quick, get behind Worm!" Drake yelled to his friends.

The three Dragon Masters ducked behind Worm as the Earth Dragon's body began to glow. A wall of green energy appeared in front of him, protecting them and the other dragons.

The powers of these Dragon Masters remind me of Eko, the master of the Thunder Dragon, Drake thought. *Eko learned how to tap into the powers of her dragon. They made her very strong.*

Drake called out to the Naga's Dragon Masters, "Please don't attack. We are not here to hurt you. We are here to warn you!"

"Intruders are not allowed in the temple," the boy and girl repeated. They glared at Drake and the others. "GO AWAY!"

They raised their arms again, preparing to attack.

URI AND ZELDA

"Worm, keep the shield up," Drake said. He turned to Jean and Darma.

"What should we do?" he asked.

"I could ask Argent to use his shine powers," Jean suggested. "That would stop them."

Drake shook his head. "We can't do that. It might hurt them," he pointed out. "We need to show these Dragon Masters that we are here to help."

"Drake? Drake? Are you there, Drake?" a familiar voice called.

The voice came from the magic mirror in his pocket. He took it out and saw Griffith's face looking at him.

"Maldred is free!" the wizard cried. "He is on his way to the temple. You must stop him from gaining control of the Naga!"

Drake held up the mirror.

"Griffith, the Naga's Dragon Masters don't believe us," he said. "Please tell them!"

The boy and girl stared at the mirror.

"Listen to these Dragon Masters!" Griffith said. "They are there to help you save the world."

"A bad wizard is coming for the Naga!" Drake added.

The Naga's Dragon Masters looked at each other. They lowered their hands.

"We believe you now," the boy said. "I am Uri."

"And I am his twin sister, Zelda," said the girl. "We are sorry we attacked you."

Drake tucked the mirror into his belt. Worm's shield of protection disappeared. Uri and Zelda walked toward them.

"How does this wizard plan to control the Naga?" Zelda asked.

Darma answered her. "He has the Silver Key and the Gold Key," he explained. "Legend says that whoever unlocks the power of the Naga can control him. That is Maldred's plan!"

Uri and Zelda gazed behind them at a huge door in the temple wall shaped like a circle. There was a dragon carved onto the face of the stone door. A dragon's body curved around the door. And a dragon head statue looked down from the very top.

Uri placed his hand on the stone door. "The Naga rests beyond this door. He is at peace in his home, deep inside the earth."

"For years, the two keys were the only way to open the door and control the Naga," Zelda said.

"But then things changed," Uri continued. "The Dragon Stone chose two Dragon Masters for the Naga."

"The Naga's Dragon Masters have kept watch over him for a very long time," Zelda said. "We are the latest ones to do so."

"There is nothing that can break our connection to the Naga," Uri finished. "Not even a powerful wizard."

Jean frowned. "You don't know Maldred," she said.

Drake had a question. "When we first saw you, you were floating in a ball of energy. Were you tapping into the Naga's powers?"

Uri smiled. "Yes, we were connecting with the Naga," he said.

"The Naga's energy is so strong that it lifts us off our feet," Zelda explained.

Uri stepped forward. "Thank you for warning us about the dark wizard, but you can leave now."

"You don't understand!" Jean said. "Maldred has powerful magic. He will find a way to —"

Boom!

As Jean spoke, a ball of dark red energy appeared out of nowhere and exploded right next to them!

MALDRED'S POWERS

"It's Maldred!" Drake yelled.

The wizard stepped out of a cloud of red smoke. He wore a patch over one eye and had a long black beard streaked with white.

"Argent, blast him with your silver shine!" Jean yelled.

"Hema, attack!" Darma commanded.

Drake knew that the Silver and Gold dragons were both really powerful. Besides using his silver shine, Argent could also reflect an opponent's attack back at them. Hema could change into any form as well as shoot gold attack beams from her eyes.

Argent and Hema began to glow with energy. Before they could attack, Maldred blasted them with magic.

The red orbs bounced off of Argent's silver shine.

Maldred dodged the return attack and pointed at the Dragon Masters.

"Worm, protect us!" Drake cried.

Worm created an energy shield in front of Drake, Darma, and Jean. Maldred's dark magic bounced off the shield.

Behind Maldred, Uri and Zelda began to glow with yellow light.

They are starting to channel the Naga's power! Drake realized. *Maybe they can stop Maldred if we can't!*

Maldred glared at the Dragon Masters protected by the shield. "Nice try, but you can't stop me!" he taunted. "Your wizards couldn't even keep me in their silly magical dimension!"

Maldred swirled around and shot two blasts of magic at Argent. The dragon spread his silver wings. The red balls of magic bounced right off the wings and zoomed back toward Maldred. The wizard held out both hands, and the balls of magic exploded before they could hit him.

"Hema, attack!" Darma cried.

Hema shot gold beams at Maldred. He pushed those back, too.

Drake sent a message to Worm. *Worm, can you stop Maldred?*

Worm closed his eyes. Using the power of his mind, he began to lift Maldred up in the air.

Maldred grinned. "I knew that you all would try to stop me," he said. "That is why, after I left wizard's prison, I invented this."

He tossed a small, glowing red bottle onto the floor.

Worm's green light began to flow out of his body and into the bottle! So did Argent's silver shine and Hema's golden glow.

Worm lost his hold on Maldred. The wizard dropped to the floor.

"What is happening?" Jean cried. She ran toward the bottle.

Before she could grab it, it zoomed up and into Maldred's hand. He put a stopper in it and tucked it into his pocket.

"All your dragons are now powerless!" he exclaimed.

UNLOCKING THE DOOR

"Worm, has Maldred really stolen your powers?" Drake asked his dragon.

It is true, Worm answered. *My powers are gone.*

"Argent, attack!" Jean yelled. But the Silver Dragon looked at her and shook his head. Jean's Dragon Stone glowed.

"Argent says his powers are gone, too!" she cried.

"It is no use," Darma said. "All our dragons' powers are trapped in Maldred's magic red bottle."

Maldred laughed. "I win! Now stand down, or I will feed you to the Naga when I summon him."

"You will never control the Naga!" the twins yelled, raising their arms.

Boom! They blasted Maldred with yellow energy. The energy formed a bubble around the wizard, trapping him.

The twins turned to Drake and the others.

"We told you," said Uri.

"We did not need your help," Zelda said.

But then . . . *POP!* The yellow bubble around Maldred exploded in a flash of red. Maldred's laugh rang through the temple as the red smoke cleared again.

"I told you that no one could stop me," he said.

Uri and Zelda stared at him, wide-eyed.

They were not expecting that! Drake guessed.

The dark wizard walked toward the round door that led to the Naga's home. He held up two discs — the Silver Key and the Gold Key.

"Fly, keys, fly, into the dragon's eyes!" Maldred chanted, and the keys flew out of his hands.

Jean climbed onto Argent's back, and they charged at Maldred. Argent swiped at him with his wing, knocking Maldred down.

But it was too late. Both keys floated up to the top of the door, where the head of a dragon was carved into the stone. The Silver Key slid into the dragon's left eye. The Gold Key slid into the dragon's right eye.

Both eyes lit up with shimmering silver and gold light – and the door opened!

The twins turned, their bodies stiff, and faced Maldred. Gold and silver light swirled in their eyes.

"We shall obey you now," they said. "You have unlocked the power of the Naga. You can control the Naga through us."

Drake looked at Jean and Darma.

"Oh no!" he said. "Uri was wrong. Their connection to the Naga was *not* stronger than the keys!"

"Uri! Zelda! Don't listen to Maldred!" Jean yelled.

But the twins stared at the dark wizard. "What is your command?" they asked.

Maldred grinned. "I command you to summon the Naga!"

THE EARTHQUAKE DRAGON

Uri and Zelda began to chant.

"Naga-avadi. Naga-avadi. Naga-avadi. Naga-avadi."

"Uri! Zelda! Don't listen to him!" Drake yelled.

"I don't think they can help it," Darma said. "The keys' powers are very strong."

"Well, we are strong, too," Jean said. She ran over to Maldred and drew her sword.

"Stop this right now!" she cried.

Maldred waved his hand, and the sword flew out of hers and stuck into the temple wall.

"The Earthquake Dragon is coming!" Maldred crowed. "Nothing you do now will stop that from happening!"

Drake knew that the Naga had caused earthquakes when he first hatched. He remembered what Griffith had told him. *He brought down mountains. He caused great floods.*

"We can't let Maldred control the Naga!" Drake said. He closed his eyes. *Worm, what can we do?*

Worm replied: *To stop Maldred, you must stop Uri and Zelda.*

Drake turned to Jean and Darma.

"Worm says we need to stop Uri and Zelda in order to stop Maldred," Drake told them.

"How can we do that without hurting them?" Jean asked. She eyed her sword stuck in the wall.

"We can't," Darma said.

Uri and Zelda continued to chant.

"Naga-avadi. Naga-avadi. Naga-avadi. Naga-avadi."

As they chanted, rows and rows of scales slid past the round door opening. Finally, a huge yellow eye appeared.

Drake gasped. "The Naga is . . . is enormous!" he stammered.

“Yes, he is,” Maldred said, with glee in his voice. He made a circle with his hands, and an image of a dragon curled up inside the earth appeared in the air. Energy lines extended from the dragon to every part of the planet.

“The Naga’s energy is connected to every place in the world,” Maldred said. “When the Naga turns his eye to a place, the earth there shakes.” Then he clapped his hands, and the image vanished.

“What shall we ask of the Naga?” the twins asked.

Maldred cackled. “Tell the Naga to turn his eye to the Kingdom of Bracken!” he commanded.

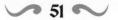

BRACKEN FALLS

"Naga, turn your eye to the Kingdom of Bracken," the twins repeated.

"Not Bracken!" Drake yelled. "No!"

The dragon's large yellow eye looked at Uri and Zelda. But the twins stared blankly ahead, still under Maldred's control.

The Naga is a peaceful dragon, Worm told Drake. *He does not want to harm anyone. But he must obey his masters.*

The Naga's eye turned away from the door.

"Let us see what is happening in Bracken now," Maldred said. "Drake, I sense that you have a magical object with you. An object that acts as a portal to Bracken."

"Portal?" Drake asked. Then he understood.

Drake held up the magic mirror.

"Excellent!" Maldred said. "Gaze into it and tell me what you see."

Drake didn't want to obey Maldred. But he needed to see what was happening in Bracken. His family, his friends – were they safe?

Drake gazed into the mirror, and a scene appeared. He could see King Roland's castle in the distance. He could see the green fields where crops grew, and the hut where his family lived. The sun was shining as villagers worked in the fields.

Then, suddenly, the ground began to shake. People began to run. Some of the huts collapsed. Big cracks in the earth started to break apart the fields.

"No! That's my home!" Drake yelled. Tears ran down his cheeks.

Darma stepped up to Maldred. "Why must you destroy the world?"

Maldred cackled. "I am not trying to destroy it. I am trying to control it," he replied. "With the power of the Naga at my command, everyone will do what I say! And I'm starting with Bracken, because that is where my enemies have gathered! Those wizards will be sorry they tried to mess with me!"

Jean pulled her sword out of the wall.

"Aaaaaaaaaaaah!" With a mighty cry, she charged toward Maldred.

The wizard scowled. He held up his hand and then pushed forward.

Magical energy sent Jean flying backward across the temple!

DRAKE'S PLAN

Jean crashed into the temple wall and slid down to the floor. Drake and Darma ran over and knelt down beside her.

"Are you all right?" Drake asked.

Jean slowly opened her eyes.

"I'm okay," Jean replied. "Just some – ow! – bumps and bruises."

The attack on Bracken had ended.

"Hmm." Maldred walked over to Drake and looked into the mirror. "Your castle is still standing. Perhaps I should make the Naga attack Bracken again? Or shall I attack somewhere else next?"

The dark wizard strolled away, stroking his beard as he paced the floor of the temple.

The Naga's eye appeared in the doorway as he waited for his next command.

Think! Drake told himself. *There has to be a way to get the twins to stop obeying him!*

His eyes traveled up to the glowing eyes of the stone dragon above the Naga's door. A solution hit him.

Drake quickly whispered to Jean and Darma, "If I can take the keys out of the eyes, Maldred won't be able to control the twins anymore. I'm going to climb up there and grab them."

Darma nodded.

"Go!" Jean urged him.

Maldred was still pacing, deciding where to attack next. Drake tiptoed to the doorway. The keys were up high on top of the door, inside the eye sockets of the stone dragon. Luckily, the carved body of the dragon along the sides of the door was perfect for climbing.

Drake climbed until he was in arm's reach of the Gold Key.

I just need to grab it and then grab the Silver Key next, he thought. *Unlocking the keys should disrupt Maldred's hold over Uri and Zelda.*

He gripped the top of the dragon's head with one hand. He stuck out his other hand to grab the Gold Key.

"Ouch!" Drake cried. The key had shocked his fingertips when he touched it!

Maldred heard him and spun around.

"What are you doing up there?" he asked.

Then he aimed his magical fingers at Drake, ready to attack.

DRAKE'S SWORD

"Leave Drake alone, you evil wizard!" Jean cried.

Maldred was still facing Drake, preparing to attack. Jean ran up to him and kicked him behind the knees. The wizard fell forward.

Darma ran to help Jean hold Maldred down. "Hurry, Drake!" he called up. "Grab the key!"

"I can't touch it!" Drake cried, but then he remembered his sword.

He used his free hand to pull the sword from his belt. His other hand slipped, but he caught the dragon's mouth before he fell. Then he used the sword to shimmy the Gold Key from the eye socket above the door.

The key dropped to the floor with a clatter!

Drake lost his grip again, and this time he fell. Worm's tail caught him before he hit the floor.

Drake scrambled to pick up the Gold Key.

"Look at the twins!" Darma yelled as he and Jean struggled to hold Maldred.

The twins were blinking, like they had just woken up. The silver and gold light had left their eyes.

Removing one key must have broken Maldred's hold on them! Drake realized.

"Uri, Zelda, you control the Naga again!" he yelled. "Tell your dragon not to hurt anybody!"

Maldred wrestled away from Jean and Darma and jumped to his feet.

"No!" the wizard fumed. "Obey me!"

"You cannot tell us what to do anymore," Uri said.

"We will tell the Naga to return to his peaceful home in the center of the earth," Zelda added.

The big yellow eye turned toward the twin Dragon Masters. A large tear glistened there.

Their Dragon Stones began to glow.

Maldred spun around and glared at Drake. "Give me that Gold Key!" he yelled.

The dark wizard charged at Drake, but Jean lunged at him again, this time grabbing him by the ankles. Then Darma grabbed the red bottle from Maldred's pocket — the bottle containing their dragons' powers!

"Dragons, get ready!" Darma cried, and he pulled out the bottle's stopper.

BACK IN THE BOTTLE

Swirls of green, silver, and gold poured from the bottle and zoomed around the temple.

Green energy swirled back into Worm.

Silver energy swirled back into Argent.

Gold energy swirled back into Hema.

"It doesn't matter how powerful your dragons are," Maldred said. "You could not stop me before, and you will not stop me now!"

"Oh, yes we will!" Drake shouted.

Every Dragon Master's stone began to glow green.

"Stop Maldred!" the five Dragon Masters commanded together.

Worm lifted Maldred into the air with the power of his mind.

"I am more powerful than your dragons!" Maldred thundered. He held up his hands, and red magic sizzled in his palms. But just as he was about to attack –

Argent blasted Maldred with his silver shine.

Hema blasted Maldred with gold beams.

The Naga's yellow eye blinked. Then a huge beam of yellow light shot out and hit Maldred.

The energy of the four dragons swirled around Maldred.

"Stop this now!" Maldred fumed. He tried to hurl an attack at the dragons, but the red energy fizzled out. "I said, STOP!"

The green, gold, silver, and yellow lights got brighter. They swirled faster and faster around Maldred. The wizard began to spin – faster, and faster, and faster.

"What should we do now? Our dragons can't hold Maldred like this forever!" Drake yelled to his friends over the loud, spinning winds.

Then he heard Griffith's voice coming from the mirror tucked into his belt.

"Drake! Drake!"

Drake looked into the mirror and saw Griffith's face – and his friends Bo and Ana next to the wizard.

"You have caught Maldred just in time! The new spell is ready! We will finish Maldred for good," Griffith said. He showed Drake his hand, which held a mound of glittering powder. "Quick, turn the mirror toward Maldred!"

Drake obeyed. The wizard was still spinning, caught up in the dragons' powers. The glittering powder streamed from the mirror and surrounded Maldred.

The Dragon Masters watched as the powder swirled with Maldred. His body transformed into hundreds of buzzing red flies!

Darma held out the empty bottle, and the flies flew right into it. Darma sealed it with the stopper.

The others gathered around Darma. They stared at the bottle.

"Good work!" Griffith called out from the mirror.

"Did your spell just turn Maldred into a bunch of flies?" Jean asked.

"Yes," Griffith replied. "Now it is up to the five of you to make sure Maldred *never* returns."

The mirror went dark.

An angry buzzing sound came from the bottle. Uri and Zelda stared at it.

"How can we make sure he won't escape?" they asked.

"That's a good question," Drake said. "But you heard Griffith. We must make sure that Maldred never returns!"

BALANCE

"We should store the bottle where no one will ever be able to find it," Jean suggested.

Uri and Zelda looked at each other.

"We know a very safe place," they said.

Zelda took the red bottle from Darma. She and Uri approached the open door.

"Naga, guard this for us," they said.

The yellow eye blinked. Then the eye moved away from the doorway. Rows and rows of scales slid past the opening. Finally, the Dragon Masters saw the tip of the Naga's tail.

Zelda held out the bottle, and the Naga folded its thick tail around it. Then the tail moved away and the Naga's eye returned to the doorway.

"Thank you, Naga," Zelda said.

"Now we must remove the Silver Key and close the door," Uri said.

"That reminds me — here's your Gold Key," Drake said, and he handed it to Darma.

Darma looked up at the Gold Dragon. "Hema, please retrieve the other key."

The Gold Dragon glowed and then transformed into a monkey. The gold monkey scrambled up and removed the Silver Key.

The Naga's huge yellow eye blinked. Then the stone door slid closed.

"The Naga is at peace again," the twins said.

The monkey climbed down and handed the Silver Key to Jean. Then Hema transformed back into a dragon.

"Now that everything is in balance, I must return to Suvarna," Darma said. "I must guard the Gold Key once more."

"And I must return to Gallia, to guard the Silver Key," Jean said.

Drake hugged his two friends. "I will miss you. But maybe Worm and I will come visit sometime."

"I hope you do," Darma said with a smile.

"Anytime," Jean said. "I still owe you a sword-fighting lesson."

Jean and Darma left with their dragons. Drake stared for a moment at the Naga's closed door.

Uri and Zelda smiled at Drake.

"Thank you for helping us defeat Maldred, Drake," Uri said.

"We could not have done it ourselves," added Zelda.

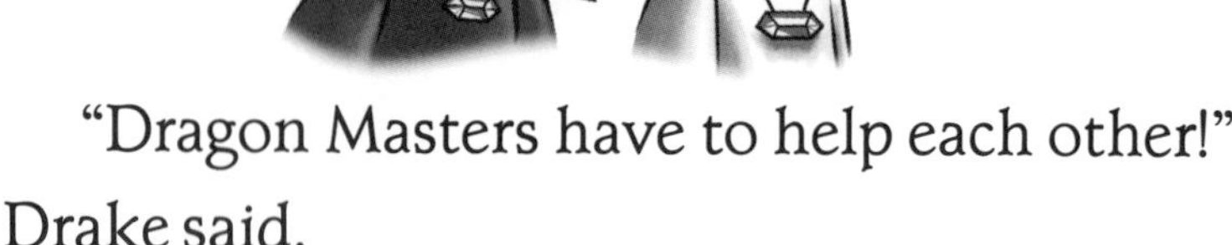

"Dragon Masters have to help each other!" Drake said.

"We should help you rebuild your home," Zelda said.

"Yes," Uri agreed. "The Naga did not mean to harm it."

"Bracken!" Drake cried. He held up the mirror. "Griffith! Is everyone okay?"

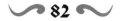

“Things are under control here,” the wizard replied. “Uri and Zelda can stay with the Naga. But you and Worm should come home right away.”

“We will,” Drake promised.

“Please come back and visit,” Uri said.

“Yes, please do,” Zelda added.

“I have an idea,” Drake said, and he handed Zelda his magic mirror. “Use this to contact us whenever you want to. Especially if there is another threat to the Naga.”

“We promise,” Uri and Zelda said.

Drake touched Worm’s wing. “Worm, let’s go home!”

AFTER THE QUAKE

Drake and Worm appeared in front of King Roland's castle in a flash of green light. All around the castle, trees had toppled down. In the village, he could see that many huts had fallen apart.

Rori ran up to him. "Drake! Worm! Let me take you to Griffith," she said. "Bo is putting out fires with Shu. And Ana and Kepri are helping villagers move into the castle."

They ran into the castle entry, past the guards. People from the village were streaming in through the gates.

"Why is everybody coming here?" Drake asked.

"King Roland says villagers can stay here until their homes are rebuilt," Rori replied. "Luckily, none of the people of Bracken got hurt during the earthquake. Thanks to the wizards."

"Really? What happened?" Drake asked.

"Griffith heard through the mirror that the Naga was going to attack Bracken," she said. "So the wizards cast a spell to protect the people. It was a really powerful spell, so it has left the wizards pretty weak."

Rori led Drake to the castle's main dining hall, which had been transformed into a hospital. Rows of beds had been set up for the wizards.

Drake left Worm outside the door and walked in. Griffith smiled when he saw Drake.

"Good work, Drake!" Griffith said, walking up to them. "I am very proud of you."

I don't feel proud of myself, Drake thought. He sighed and said, "I just wish we had saved Bracken."

Then he heard a voice behind him. "Drake!"

Drake's mother ran toward him. She crushed him in a big hug.

"Oh, Drake, I've been so worried about you," his mom said.

Drake started to cry. "I'm so glad you're okay," he said.

She nodded. "Thanks to the wizards, nobody was hurt," she said. "But many homes have been lost, and the fields are destroyed."

"The crops are ruined?" he asked.

Drake came from a family of onion farmers. He knew how important the crops were to the kingdom.

She nodded. "Yes. They're all gone."

Drake turned to Griffith. "Can you use magic to bring the crops back?"

The wizard shook his head. "That will take a different kind of power. I'm afraid —" Then his eyes lit up. "Ah, Petra!"

Drake turned to see a blond-haired girl walk in with a four-headed green dragon. It was Petra and her Poison Dragon, Zera.

Petra rushed over to them.

"Griffith!" she cried. "I found the special book you wanted in my family's library. You were right! There is a dragon in the Land of Inis Banba. A dragon with the power to heal the land!"

"Excellent!" Griffith replied. "You have arrived just in time!"

Drake looked at his mom and smiled. "There is hope."

Petra leafed through the book. "The book says that the Spring Dragon is very difficult to find."

"It won't be easy," Griffith agreed.

"We have to try," Drake said. "We need to find this dragon and save Bracken!"

TRACEY WEST lives in the misty mountains of New York state, where it is easy to imagine dragons roaming free in the green hills. She shares her home with her husband, one very hungry cat, two dogs, and a bunch of chickens. She is also the stepmom to three grownup kids.

Becoming a children's book writer has been a dream of hers since she was a little girl. She has written dozens of books since she had that dream. If she wasn't a children's book writer, she would probably be a wizard.

DANIEL GRIFFO lives in Argentina with his wife, Elba, and their two children, Valentina and Benjamin. As a child, Daniel loved creating and drawing pictures. He worked hard to develop his artistic skills. At the age of seventeen, he got his first illustration job and then he gained experience working for several large companies. Daniel looks at each project as a new adventure. He always enjoys exploring the wonderful world of illustration.

DRAGON MASTERS

EYE OF THE EARTHQUAKE DRAGON

Questions and Activities

What makes Dragon Masters Uri and Zelda so powerful? Reread pages 26 and 32.

Griffith gives Drake a magic mirror. What powers does this mirror have? Look back on pages 15, 53, and 76.

How does the Naga create earthquakes? Reread page 51.

In Chapter 13, the Dragon Masters use Griffith's glittering powder. What does the powder do to Maldred?

Write and draw what **YOU** think will happen next with Maldred. Make sure to use the words "first," "then," and "finally" to guide your story.

scholastic.com/branches